Retirement Killer

On The Hunt, Volume 3

Samuel Davies

Published by S L Davies, 2023.

RETIREMENT KILLER

First edition. June 8, 2023.

ISBN: 979-8223134909

Written by Samuel Davies.

Table of Contents

Prologue

Edward Troyer

"I'm sorry for your loss, Mr. and Mrs. Troyer," the coroner said as he sat opposite my wife in a small meeting room. "Was your mother diabetic?"

I frowned and shook my head. "No. Not at all."

Dean, the coroner's frown deepened. "So, she had no reason to have insulin in her system?"

"Not that I would be aware of. I was with her at her last appointment, and there was no talk of insulin or diabetes. Why has something come up in her autopsy?"

Dean breathed in deeply before slowly letting it out. "I'm afraid so. I've contacted the Homicide Unit at Melbourne Precinct."

I gasped, and my eyes widened. "My mother was murdered?"

Dean winced. "Without a thorough investigation, I can't say for sure. However, I know your mother had a lot of insulin in her system. And that was the cause of her death. With you telling me that she wasn't known to be diabetic, and I didn't find anything in her paperwork that said she had diabetes, it makes me question how she had the insulin in her system."

"Oh my god," my wife Amanda cried. "That's awful. It has to be the nursing home. Mum said that many of her friends had been dying suspiciously."

I nodded my head. "Have you looked into Silver Lake Nursing Home?"

"Yes, this is why I have contacted the Homicide Unit, particularly the Serial Killer Unit. Your mother was right when she said several suspicious deaths were coming out of Silver Lake."

"Jesus," I groaned. Mum was old and was slowly starting into dementia. She could no longer walk, and I couldn't care for her because I had a family and couldn't give up work. Not that it had matter, Mum, I'd discovered, had booked herself in to see the facility and decided that she would go there. All in all, the transition into nursing care had been easy.

Mum said that she didn't want to be a burden. She felt it was selfish to expect me to give up work or for Amanda to take time away from the kids. With Dad long gone, Mum decided the best thing for her was to go into nursing care. So, within a few weeks, we had the house on the market, and Mum moved into a room she was sharing with another lady.

They became fast friends. Tabatha was Dutch, and the two spent hours discussing growing up in their home countries. Tabatha was younger than Mum but had lost her legs due to diabetes. Apparently, she hadn't been pleased when her kids had put her in Silver Lake, but once she and Mum became friends, she seemed happier with the decision.

At first, I just thought maybe Mum was perhaps reading into things when she said that people were dying and that she felt someone was killing them. I thought it might have been dementia. But then I received a call from the nursing home three days telling me Mum had died. Tabatha died the night before. It was beyond suspicious. I'd demanded an autopsy because I didn't believe she had just passed of old age. I'm glad I did. Now I was sitting here discovering that my mother and her best friend were possibly the victims of a serial killer.

"Maverick Wolfe and his partner Harris Bishop are two detectives that run the Serial Killer Unit out of Melbourne; they are currently conducting interviews with all of the families whose parents have died suspiciously at Silver Lake. I suspect that they will be in contact with you in a day or two."

I breathed out a steady breath. "Thank you, Dean. When will Mum's body be released to us?"

"Today," Dean replied with a warm smile. "I've done all the tests I can do and signed off on her death certificate."

I nodded and stood with Amanda by my side. I reached out to shake the coroners, who had kept me informed.

"I appreciate all that you've done."

Dean smiled. "When you have made an appointment with a funeral home, we will be able to release your mother to their care, and they will take over from there."

"We will be going through Cottonwood Funeral Home."

Dean smiled again. "They are very professional and caring."

"Thank you again, Dean," I said as I took my wife's hand and led us out of the coroner's building. My heart was heavy, and a large dark cloud hung over me. As an only child, I had to bear this on my own. I knew there would be a day I would have to bury my only living parent, but I never suspected it would be because she was murdered.

My phone buzzed just as I climbed into the car, and I saw that it was an unknown number. "Hello?"

"Hello, Edward Troyer?"

"Yes, speaking."

"Hello, Edward; I'm sorry to call you at what must be a painful time. My name is Detective Maverick Wolfe, and I am from the Homicide Unit in Melbourne. I'm wondering if there would be a time that we can visit with you to discuss the passing of your mother, Amzi Troyer?"

"Of course. I've just finished meeting with Dean Richards. He told me that I could expect a call from you. My wife and I are about to go home now, so any time this afternoon would be great."

I gave the detective my address and ended the call. Glancing over at Amanda, my heart filled with love. She had been a complete rock for me. I don't know how I would cope if I didn't have her by my side.

"I love you," I said with a smile.

Amanda's eyes welled with happiness as she reached out a soft hand and skimmed it across my cheek. "I love you too, Edward. We will get through this together."

I kissed Amanda's hand and nodded my head. We would. We will get through this and fight every step to get justice for my mum.

Chapter One

Maverick

"That is eight suspicious deaths from Silver Lake Nursing Home," I said as I scrubbed my hand over my chin and looked at the board that held the photos of the elderly patients Dean had marked as suspicious.

"All the same cause of death?" Nathan questioned.

"Yes, all had excessive amounts of insulin in their system, and all but one, Joey Nangle, had no earlier medical history of diabetes. And Joey's diabetes was being controlled with Metformin and diet."

"Can Dean tell the difference between the insulin that was given?" Paola asked.

I shook my head. "No. All it shows is that the patient had a large amount of insulin in their system. In fact, the only reason Dean even started testing for it was that he had many patients coming to him from Silver Lake Nursing Home."

"Oh, so there could be even more?" Harris gasped.

I nodded my head. "Yep. Dean said that when he reviewed his records, he had had sixty-seven deaths from nursing homes in the last three years. With Covid, it's not unusual that the deaths would be up, but he said those sixty-seven weren't as a result of Covid. He plans to go back and test all of the blood stored from those patients."

"He keeps blood samples?" Nathan asked.

"Not normally, but something in his gut had told him to keep these samples. He said he hadn't realized why until now."

"Thank god he did; who knows how many others we have missed. Shit, Maverick, this could be huge," Charlee said with a shake of her head.

"That's what worries me. If someone purposely overdoses the elderly, who knows how long they have been at it and how many they have successfully killed that can never be proven."

"So, what do we know? I'm assuming we are probably looking at either a doctor, nurse, or orderly," Harris said.

I nodded. "All of these patients that we know for sure died of an insulin overdose within a month of one another. I've contacted Haley Reynolds, the nursing director of Silver Lake, and she is, along with their legal team, pulling all patient files of the deceased and employees' files. We want to look particularly closely at those employees working with our victims at the time of their deaths."

"When can we expect them?" Landyn asked.

"I've already got the patient files, but I think the legal team might be holding up the patient files for privacy. Derek is working with Monica in getting them subpoenaed so that they have to give us them."

"Weird that they so readily gave over the patient files," Harris mused.

I chuckled. "Yeah, those were the ones I expected to fight for. But they handed them over pretty much at once. I wasn't sure if that meant Haley gave them without the legal team's input. But it is a good start."

"Who are our victims?" Paola asked.

I walked over to the board and pointed at the first picture. "This is victim one. Matilda O'Murphy was seventy-two years old. Her records state that she had dementia brought on by alcohol abuse. She'd been in the nursing home for only three weeks when she died. The nurse on duty found her on the floor; her heart was no longer beating; they tried CPR but could not revive her. That was why she was sent for an autopsy initially to discover if the fall had caused the death. Dean hadn't even finished her autopsy when the second victim died," I moved over to the second photo and tapped on the wall.

"This is Esme Morrissey, Esme was sixty-nine years old."

"Jesus, sixty-nine is young to be in a nursing home," Charlee exclaimed.

I nodded. "Yeah, I thought that too. But Esme had no children and had never married. Apparently, she'd presented at the hospital with severe burns on her arms and legs from dropping a boiling pot of water on herself. She was sent home only to have the wounds become infected and was rushed back to the hospital with sepsis, the decision was taken out of her hands, and she was placed into nursing care. She'd been at Silver Lake for a little over six months. Esme died the day after Matilda; they had been roommates. It was Esme that had raised the alarm about Matilda falling out of the bed."

"And she died the same way?" Nathan queried.

"Yep, insulin overdose. The next three patients all died on the same night, Robin Hartigan, Andrew Martin, and William Hickey. Robin and Andrew shared a room while William was in the room beside them. Robin was eighty-four, Andrew was seventy-nine, and William was ninety-eight. All had been completely healthy, even at ninety-eight, until suddenly dying within minutes of one another. These three started to raise the alarm bells for Dean and Haley."

"Haley never contacted homicide?" Charlee asked.

"Not that I'm aware of. She made the statement when I spoke to her that she wanted to do an internal investigation first."

Charlee hummed, and I could see that she wasn't impressed. I'd felt the same way when I spoke to Haley, and she stated that she hadn't directly brought it to the police's attention. In fact, we didn't hear about it until Dean reported it himself.

"The following victim died two days later: Joey Nangle, who was ninety-two. As I said, he did have a history of type two diabetes and was being controlled by Metformin and diet. However, he still had far too much insulin in his system, so Dean felt that he, too, had been overdosed purposely. The morning after Joey died, the nursing staff discovered

Major Marcell's body in bed; he was eighty-eight. At first, the nursing staff tried to pass him off as a Covid patient. And while Dean could see that he had Covid, that wasn't what had killed him. Like the others, he had an overdose of insulin in his system. Then there were three days when there were no deaths, but Isaac Byler died on the fourth. He was eighty-eight years old. Then the following day was when Tabatha Blough was discovered dead. She was seventy-six. Our final victim died yesterday and was Tabatha's roommate. Her name was Amzi Troyer. She was eighty-two years old. Her son Edward said his mother was a strong woman and showed no signs of being ill. She'd had Covid and survived with nothing more than a sniffle. So, for her to simply up and die struck him as suspicious. As it does me. So, that's our victims. Now we just have to find our suspect."

Chapter Two

K iller
        I'd seen the coroner speaking to Haley. It was going to be time to move on. It wasn't that I wanted to kill. I actually had tried to save them. These people, it was sad. They were losing their minds. They were just shells existing. That was no way to live. The thought of being stuck in a nursing home while people did everything for me, including wiping my ass when I shit myself was horrifying. It was the most undignified way to age.

I'd heard all of their stories. The men and women at this nursing home came from worldwide. Some of them soldiers, having fought and survived two world wars. Some teachers, doctors, all different careers. All had a long life of stories. And by the time they reached the nursing home, most of those stories were forgotten. Half the time, the people didn't even know who they were anymore.

They no longer recognized those they loved. Mothers would forget their children, and husbands would forget their wives. It wasn't enjoyable. In fact, I couldn't help but think that Dementia and Alzheimer's were the cruelest way to die. A person lives doing great things, only to forget everything and become utterly incapable of caring for themselves in the last of their years.

So, I didn't see myself as a killer. I was a savior. I was saving these people from having to spend however long, slowly becoming something they weren't. I gave them dignity in a quick death. I saved their families the heartache of watching their parents waste away to nothing. Of course, a loved one dying was always hard, but watching them slowly forget everything they once knew was worse.

I should know. I cared for my ailing mother for twenty-seven years. I watched her waste away. Always a solid-built woman, she became small and fragile. Her skin would bruise and be almost transparent. Tiny germs that filled the air made her sick. Her body couldn't move as she once did, and she relied on me to carry her to the bathroom and clean her when she'd soiled herself.

Slowly she started to lose her memory; at first, she would call me her sister's name. Then she would think I was a stranger. At times terror took over her face when she saw me and thought I was there to rob her. It tore at me and broke me down. Of course, I never let anyone know how painful it was and how hard it had been. No, I'd smile and say Mum was doing fine. All the while cursing aging and hating every minute of it. With every piece of memory Mum lost, it was another slice to my heart, making me colder and more determined to save older people from the same fate.

When Mum finally passed away, it was a relief. I felt so guilty for being pleased that she was finally at rest. But I was pleased. She didn't hurt anymore, she didn't have the worry or concern, she didn't need to fear. I wanted to bring that same peace to other families.

However, I also wasn't stupid. I knew what I was doing was wrong. I knew that killing people was illegal and immoral, even though I was doing it to be helpful. It meant I had to be always cautious of where I worked and how often I took a life. It had become a bit of a thrill to me, and I'd got sloppy. I'd taken too many lives too quickly, and now I would have to move on to another nursing facility.

I sighed as I clocked out of work for the last time. I didn't bother telling anyone that I wasn't coming back. They wouldn't find me anyway. I made sure to never give my real name or where I really lived. Everything about me was fake. Even my credentials as a nurse.

Everything I knew about nursing I picked up from caring for Mum. With a heavy heart, I climbed into my car and brought it to life. I was wealthy. I had nice cars and a fancy house, but it all meant nothing when my heart ached the way it did.

It ached with regret that I couldn't help more families. I'd petitioned the government for years to instate euthanasia for everyone. I was excited when they finally passed the laws in Australia. But then I read the conditions. A person could only have aided dying if they were going to die in the next twelve months. It was cruel to leave these people alive. We were allowed to put down animals when they got too old to cope; why couldn't we do the same for older people.

Sighing as I pulled into my long driveway, I looked up at the enormous house I'd inherited from my mother's estate. It was a huge, ostentatious house that was all about show than comfort. Hell, I only used three rooms in the damned place. The rest was locked away, gathering dust. I thought about selling it, but it was all I had left of Mum.

Dad had died years earlier during the Vietnam War. Mum was pregnant with me, and she'd never bothered to remarry. Instead, she chose to live off of her family's money and raise me to one day be able to care for her. I was home-schooled. It was just me and Mum. I'm confident our neighbors wouldn't have known a child had lived in this home. Not until Mum died anyway, and it was all over the news. Lucille Haugh, daughter of mining magnate Gerald Haugh, dies, leaving behind one daughter.

A daughter who would go on to kill.

Chapter Three

Harris

My heart was heavy as I walked into work. We'd been hoping like crazy that Daisy wouldn't need more treatment. But the tumor was still there. The doctors said that she would now need a round of radiation therapy. In my gut, I felt we would be going down this path, but it didn't make it easier.

The more complicated part was that I'd used all my holidays and long service on her last round of chemotherapy and had no more time off. I needed to work, Taylor had given up her job, and we couldn't afford for me to retire early from the police force. We needed the money; cancer treatment wasn't cheap. Even in Australia, where health care was better than in other countries, it was still expensive.

"Hey Harris, how'd you go at the doctor's?" Maverick asked as I flopped into the seat beside him at our desks.

"Another round, this time radiation therapy. They are going to start her tomorrow."

Maverick winced. The man had been on this journey with us, and I knew I could rely on him.

"How long is this going to be for?"

"They said five rounds."

"And will she get to ring the bell?"

I shrugged my shoulders. "I don't know, man. I'm scared. I'm scared that this cancer will beat her, Mav."

Maverick shook his head and grasped my shoulder. "No. You have a strong little girl. Please do not give up on her yet. She will beat this and go on cause you hell through her teen years. But this cancer will stand no chance."

"I hope you're right. I can't even begin to think what it would be like to lose her." My eyes welled with tears as I considered the possibility. The very thought shredded me. My daughters were the most amazing things to ever happen to me. The idea of potentially losing Daisy was like a knife to the heart.

"Don't let your brain go there, man. We have to keep focusing on the positive. I know it's hard, and you know that I'm here to shoulder your burdens. Lay them on me when it is getting too much. I've got some annual leave. I'm happy to sit with my Daisy girl for days off."

I smiled at my best brother. We might not have shared blood, but he was closer to me than a friend. He was the brother I'd always wanted and needed.

"Thanks, man. I might take you up on that; I know it will be hard on Taylor."

"Say no more; I'll let Derek know I will take some time off. In the meantime, I've got the files of all the employees from Silver Lake Nursing Home," he said as he stood from his desk and pointed at files in a folder in front of his computer.

I nodded and reached over to the folder, opening it on the desk before me. Silver Lake had seventy-eight employees; some were full-time, part-time, and casual. I glanced down the list to see if any names stood out to me, but no one I recognized.

I leaned back in the seat and tapped on my chin. We would have to review every name and see if something came back. I glanced at the list that said when the person was employed; the fact that the deaths at Silver Lake were current suggested that the employee wouldn't be one of the older people. I suspected that they would be pretty new.

I also couldn't help but think that there was a good chance that the murderer probably had worked elsewhere. My gut told me that this wasn't the first time they had killed. I'd asked Dean to provide me with any other suspicious deaths in nursing homes around Victoria that we could look into. If we could find a correlation, there would be a good chance that we would find our killer.

"Alright, I'm taking the next five weeks off, are you okay to lead this case, or do you want me to get Nathan to do it?" Maverick asked as he returned to the desk.

I looked up at him and smiled before shaking my head. "No. I'll be fine to lead it. Thank you, man; you don't know how much this means to me."

Maverick smiled down at me. "This is what family does, you know that."

I sighed and nodded. "Yeah, I do. But I still appreciate it."

Maverick gave me a wink and waved his hand to tell me everything was all good. I quickly texted Taylor to inform her that Maverick would support her at the hospital. Daisy would be thrilled to spend time with her Uncle Mav. At least this time, we didn't have to stay overnight at the hospital. However, Taylor still needed support while Daisy underwent the treatment.

Chapter Four

Nathan

"Hey, Nathan, can you come into my office momentarily?" Derek asked from the door of the SKU room.

"Sure," I replied with uncertainty. My mind started racing as I wondered why I might be in trouble with our captain.

"Come and sit down, and stop looking so worried," Derek chuckled.

I smiled nervously and took a seat opposite him. I was still relatively new to the homicide unit and had little to do with Derek. Even though he was my boss, he usually sent a message through Maverick or Harris if he wanted us to know something. He didn't typically ask to see one of us junior detectives unless we were in trouble.

"Have I done something wrong?" I asked with a quiver in my voice. I hated how nervous I got around anyone in authority. I could look any hardened criminal in the face and not bat an eyelid but sit me in front of one of the bosses, and I stressed out. My counselor said it had something to do with the fact that I was a perfectionist and people pleaser.

"Not at all," Derek replied with a warm smile that was supposed to put me at ease. It didn't do anything to settle my racing heart or my swirling belly. "I asked you in here because Maverick will take the next three weeks off to help Harris and his wife with their daughter as she goes through a round of radiation."

"Oh, okay," I replied. I knew that Harris's daughter Daisy was about to start a round of radiation therapy for her cancer. Still, I hadn't realized Maverick was also taking the time off.

Derek nodded his head. "Harris has no more paid time off and can't afford to work."

"Oh," I replied with wide eyes. "Can I give him some of mine or something? I mean, he should be there for his daughter."

Derek smiled. "That is lovely of you to offer; Nathan and I know that Harris would be appreciative; unfortunately, it doesn't work like that, and we can't do it. Otherwise, I would have given him all of mine first."

"So, what does this mean? I mean, for this case of the people in the nursing home?"

Derek nodded again and linked his fingers across his chest as he leaned back in his seat. "Well, Maverick was going to be leading the case, but because he isn't going to be here, and I suspect that Harris's mind is going to be pretty mush, I'm hoping that you will step into the role of the lead detective."

My eyes widened, and my mouth dropped open. "Are you serious?"

Derek let out a small chuckle. "Deadly."

"Oh shit, I mean, yeah, thank you."

Derek smiled warmly at me again. "You've earned this, Nathan. You're a great cop, and I'm proud to have you on my team."

I swallowed thickly as my emotions welled up inside of me. "Thank you," I croaked as I stood on shaky legs and turned from Derek's office, heading back to the SKU room.

"Hey, what did the boss man want?" Landyn asked.

"He asked me to be the lead detective on the retirement killer case."

Landyn's eyes widened before he booted out a loud laugh. "No shit? That's fucking awesome, man."

"Yep, if Mav or Harris can't do it, I wouldn't want anyone other than you to lead this case, Nath," Charlee called across the room. My cheeks blushed at the compliment, and I licked over my bottom lip before clearing my throat.

"Thanks, guys. So, I should ask where we are on the case?"

"Well, I've got a list of the employees' names that worked at Silver Lake during the deaths. Two nurses and one orderly have quit in the last two weeks. The orderly had his resignation in for a while, though, so I don't think he is guilty, but worth looking into," Paola explained.

"What about the other two nurses?"

"So, one is called Karen Barker; she is thirty-eight and didn't get along with anyone. All of the other staff that Charlee and I spoke to had nothing nice to say about her. They all said she was a bitch and sloppy."

I hummed. "That might be a good one to start with."

"That's what I was thinking," Paola answered.

"Who is the other nurse?"

"Allison Haugh. She worked her last shift the night that Amzi Troyer died and never returned, never contacted Haley or anything, just never showed up again. When Haley tried contacting her, Sophie's phone was disconnected."

I scratched at my chin. There were two suspicious nurses. It didn't mean that it was either one of them. But they were the first we would look at.

"Has Dean returned to you with other suspicious cases at nursing homes?" I asked.

"Yep," Harris said as he came into the room. His eyes were red-rimmed like he'd been crying, and his face looked aged. I could see the stress all over him. "Congratulations on being lead detective, man; you deserve it."

I smiled. "Thank you," I replied with a nod. "How is Daisy?"

Harris sighed. "She had a massive panic attack before they anesthetized her. Poor Taylor was crying, I was crying, hell, even Mav was crying. This one is rough."

"Shit, I'm so fucking sorry. If you need anything, and I mean anything, let me know. I've got some savings; I'm happy to give you if you need the money for your family so you can take time off."

Harris gave me a tight smile and shook his head. "Thank you, man, but I won't need that. Just be prepared to put up with my grumpy ass."

"Anytime," I replied. "So, you said that Dean got back to you?"

Harris cleared his throat and nodded. "Yep. There was a total of thirty-five suspicious deaths over the last twenty-one years, all in nursing homes, all unsolved. And all of them were insulin overdoses."

"Jesus."

"Yeah, I thought so too. So, how do you want to handle this?"

I rubbed the back of my neck as I thought about what we needed to do. Thirty-five deaths possibly connected to the same killer would be like a needle in a haystack.

"We have the names of the staff that currently work at Silver Lake, plus the three that have recently left; let's go through Dean's list and contact the nursing homes; I want to see if any of them have the same staff working there during the suspicious deaths. We will see if maybe we can narrow it down."

Chapter Five

K iller

"Well, Mrs. Rizzo, your resume is imposing. You've worked for some big names," the interviewer glanced over at me over the glasses she had perched on the end of her nose. Her face reminded me of a magpie, with that long nose and beady eyes, always watching and ready to pick me up on any mistake.

I wondered if I shouldn't bother trying to work at Bartholomew Central Nursing Center. I got the distinct feeling this woman would be watching me closely. The resume she was referring to was bullshit, as was my name. At every job, I had a new identity. Every reference was me on a different phone.

"I spoke with Ms. Sophie Haugh, your employer reference from Silver Lake; she said that you are a very hard worker and was highly impressed with your level of competency."

"Thank you," I replied.

"Well, I see no problem having you start; Sophie explained that you could begin immediately."

"Yes, that's correct."

"Wonderful. What if I pencil your first shift in for tomorrow afternoon, starting at three. Our afternoon shifts are always the quietest, as you would know."

"Yes, I prefer to work an afternoon shift anyway."

The woman, whose name I hadn't bothered to remember, smiled. "That's great; I always struggle to find staff willing to be away from their families for an evening. Are you a mother, Mrs. Rizzo?"

I shook my head. "No, and please call me Lisa."

"Lisa, it is. Your husband won't mind you being away."

I let out a dramatic sigh and shook my head, placing my saddest mask on my face. "I'm afraid my husband is no longer with us. He passed away several years ago."

"Oh, Lisa, I'm dreadfully sorry."

"It's okay. That is why I like to work the afternoon shift; it takes my mind off things and cures my loneliness without him."

"I completely understand. Thank you for being so open with me. I will be sure to roster you on the afternoons so you can continue doing what you're doing."

I smiled and nodded. That is another line of shit. But from the look on her face, she'd taken it hook, line, and sinker. What could I say? I was an actress. I had a mother who had been a child actress; of course, I learned from the best. She was a manipulative bitch who used her beauty and fame to her advantage. Me? I was tarred from the same brush. I got what I wanted: a bat of my eye lids, a coy smile, or unwarranted confidence. The only difference between me and my mother was that I didn't manipulate people to get the men in my bed. I manipulated them to save them.

"Lisa, it is a pleasure to meet you, and I look forward to having you as part of our team." The woman stood and stuck her hand out for me to shake. I stretched out my perfectly manicured hand and gripped hers.

I learned early on that being unassuming was the best way to get away with things. I was always dressed impeccably. My nails were perfect, and my hair was never out of place. There were never undyed roots showing through. My clothes, although expensive, were not so showy that I looked like I was dripping in money. It was an image, and the idea worked for what I wanted.

"It was lovely to meet you," I replied sweetly. "I look forward to working at Bartholomew Central."

I turned and left the office before heading toward my car. Brand new, a Mazda, in black. Bought with cash under the name of Lisa Rizzo. My latest pseudonym. One that will last me until it's time to move on. I smirked as I glanced up at the front doors of the nursing home. A vast dark brick building that loomed over the Melbourne streets. Filled with priests and nuns who had dedicated their lives to chastity.

Many were probably not as chaste as they liked to portray. Some who had done the most vile things. Those were the ones I wouldn't save. They could live a long time, rotting in their brain of evil and torture. They were the ones that I would step over. The ones I saved were those who had lived a good life. The ones that had their stories to tell yet lived, forgetting most of them. Those were the people that I saved. They deserved to have their misery ended. The others could rot for all I cared. Disgusting, vile beasts shouldn't have even been allowed to live. Yet because they did, they could live and rust in their skin until their god finally stripped away their dignity. They died lonely, broken, and forgotten in a hospital bed, stinking of bleach and medical equipment.

Chapter Six

Harris

The hardest thing I've ever had to do was leave my daughter in the hands of Taylor, Maverick, and the doctors while I walked away. Daisy was so unhappy that I couldn't stay for her treatment. I fucking hated it. I was beyond grateful that Maverick was stepping in, but it didn't change the fact that I wanted to be there for my little girl. The one thing I could be glad of was that at least this time, she got to come home after her therapy rather than stay in the hospital.

Doctors told us that this would be enough to finally eliminate the cancer. I wasn't a Christian man, but damn, I've been praying like mad in hopes that she won't need any more treatments after this. I watched my lively little girl waste away during the chemo. By all accounts, she would have a similar reaction to radiation therapy.

I glanced down the list of all the employees working with Silver Lake. Only three stood out as having left in the last few weeks. There had been no other deaths since the three staff members left. That obviously made me assume it was one of the staff, Karen Barker, Allison Haugh, and an orderly, Malcolm Lyons. I'd already cleared Malcolm; he had been working at Silver Lake since he was twenty-three years old and finally decided to take his extended service leave before retiring. So, there was no question for him.

I could see that Karen Barker had worked at several nursing homes according to her resume that Haley, the manager at Silver Lake, had sent over.

"What have you discovered?" Nathan asked as he slid into the seat opposite me.

"Not much, I'm afraid. I contacted all of the nursing homes where Karen worked at. She worked on Dean's lists of suspicious deaths for Langley Hall and Oak Mill nursing homes, but she wasn't working at either of them at the time of the deaths. Silver Lake is the only place she has worked that coincides with suspicious deaths."

Nathan hummed. "It's not to count her out, but it looks less likely. What about Allison Haugh?"

"Well, this is the one that I'm confused about. She has said she worked at Langley Hall and Oak Mill, Riverbend, Whispering Willows, and as a private nurse. She has put the references down for private nursing. However, none of them are connected numbers. When I looked the people up in the phone book, they weren't listed. Even searching for them through our databases, nothing is registered to these people. In fact, it's like they don't exist."

"That's because they don't," Landyn said as he flopped into the chair beside me. "I just got off the phone to Langley Hall. Allison Haugh has never worked there; they had never heard of her. But when the suspicious deaths were happening there, they had a Lucille Monroe working for them."

"So, we are dealing with someone using a false name?"

Landyn nodded his head. "Looks that way. When I rang Oak Mill, they said that the suspicious deaths stopped when one of the nurses left, named Jessica Phillips. It was the same story at Riverbend, where she used the name Michelle Smith, and Whispering Willows, where she used the name Natalie Parker."

"I've just found another two," Charlee announced as she joined us. "At Trinity, she was using the name Tamara Johnson; at Southern Cross, it was Margaret Davis."

"Christ," I gasped. "How many deaths are we looking at?"

"There are forty-eight nursing homes alone, but if she did private nursing as her resume says, the number could be even higher."

"Fucking hell," I spat. "We need to find this woman. Do we have a picture of her?"

"Yep, I was able to get an employee picture from Trinity. Apparently, she could skip out at all the other facilities without them realizing they hadn't taken an ID photo."

Charlee placed the color photo on the table before us, and I frowned. "Does she look familiar?" I questioned. I couldn't pinpoint it, but she looked like someone I knew. But I couldn't recall who it was.

"Yeah, she does. Is she famous?" Nathan pondered.

I hummed and shook my head. "I don't think so."

Derek walked up behind the desk and glanced down at the picture. "If I didn't know better, I'd swear that was Lucille Haugh."

"As in the actress?" I asked.

Derek nodded his head. "I was just coming over to see how you guys were getting on. Do we know who this woman is?"

"This is who we suspect is responsible for the suspicious deaths, but we don't know her real name," I explained.

"Wait a minute, she used the name Haugh at Silver Lake, and she used the name Lucille at Langley Hall," Nathan said, looking up from the picture.

"It can't be the actress she died about twenty years ago," Derek said. "I remember because my mother adored her. She'd gone to school with Lucille."

"Did Lucille have any children?" Charlee asked.

Derek hummed and stroked his fingers on his chin. "I don't know. I remember something being said when Lucille died, but I can't remember if it was a child or perhaps just a niece or nephew. Maybe look up articles from when Lucille died; there has to be something about it."

"Good idea," Charlee answered as she stood from the table and went to her computer. What would be the odds that a famous actress would produce a serial killer for a daughter?

Chapter Seven

Charlee

"Okay, so I spoke to my friend, James. He is the know-all on everything Hollywood starlets; he said Lucille Haugh had a daughter anyway. Her name was Sophie Haugh, but he seemed to think Sophie died not long after her mother," I explained to the rest of my team in the SKU room.

"So, it could be just a coincidence that this woman and Lucille Haugh look alike," Nathan mused.

"Yeah, I showed the picture to James, and he said he could have sworn that it was Sophie, but apparently, Lucille was weird. I don't know the full story because she kept it out of the spotlight, but James told me that when Lucille got pregnant, she refused to tell anyone who the father was. Then after she had the baby, she did a couple of interviews, which was it; after that, she became a complete recluse. No one heard anything more from her and knew nothing about Sophie until Lucille died. That was the first time the media had seen Sophie in all that time. Media tried to get interviews with Sophie, but she refused and ignored all phone calls."

"Oh, ok, that is weird." Nathan sighed and scrubbed his hands over his face. "I mean, it's a stretch to think that this woman is the daughter of some Hollywood star, but the resemblance is strange. But until we actually know who this woman is, we can't say for sure."

"I've run her photo through the system, and nothing has returned. From what I can tell, this woman doesn't have a license or anything," Paola stated with a frown etched into her brow.

"Charlee, can you do a bit more research into Sophie Haugh? Something about this whole thing is niggling at my gut. If you can search to see if there is a death certificate for her, maybe Dean can help, and if there isn't, perhaps there is an address."

"Sure," I replied, turning and leaving the room to ring Dean. This case was a mystery, but that was why I loved working as a cop. I'd joined the police force with one goal in mind, to become a detective. I'd always loved mystery books and television shows; it made me want to do it in real life. Of course, life wasn't always like the movies, we didn't solve the case overnight, but I loved my job and would work it twenty-four-seven if Derek let me.

"Dean Richards," the coroner answered after a few rings.

"Hi, Dean, it's Charlee Saxton from the SKU; I'm ringing regarding a case we are currently working on."

"Hey Charlee, I was just about to come and see you all; I've gathered all the files for the retirement homes that had suspicious deaths; they range back twenty years."

"Holy shit, you think it could be the same person?"

"I don't know for sure, but all of the victims had high insulin levels in their system, which is their cause of death."

"What about elderly people that weren't in a nursing home?"

"Yep, I've checked that out too. I've found five cases, which were thirteen years ago."

"Same cause of death?"

"Yep. However, only one of those cases could I not think so completely. The man had just been diagnosed with type two diabetes. But I don't think it was a doctor's error with the amount of insulin he had in his system. No doctor would prescribe that much."

I hummed. "Interesting. Anyway, I was calling to ask if it would be possible for you to look into a death record for me?"

"Sure; what is the name and date of death?"

"I don't know the date of death; I don't even know if she is dead. But her name is Sophie Haugh."

I heard Dean clicking on a keyboard before he hummed. "I can't see any death certificate for Sophie Haugh. I have her as a next of kin for a Lucille Haugh."

"Yeah, that was Sophie's mother. I'd been told that Sophie might have died shortly after Lucille."

"No, there is definitely no record of any deaths."

"Okay, thanks, Dean; I'll see you when you come in."

I ended the call and went to the computer bringing up the Google search before typing in Sophie's name. Of course, there were many old articles about her mother and questioning where Sophie was. Still, nothing told me anything about the woman. She was a bit of a mystery.

I had no idea if we were going down the right path, it might be a complete waste of time, but there had to be something. Strangely, this woman would use the surname Haugh and Lucille plus look like Sophie. It felt like it was bigger than a coincidence.

Chapter Eight

Maverick

"Oh, sweet girl, I know it hurts," I soothed as gently rocked Daisy. The poor little one's body shuddered under the weight of her tears. Big fat tears dribbled down her cheeks and dripped from her chin.

Taylor had tried to be strong, but Daisy's cries had become too much for her, and she started to cry. I'd taken Daisy out of Taylor's arms and told her to go get a coffee and that I would take over caring for Daisy. At first, Taylor didn't want to leave her, but when Daisy's sobs eased while she was in my arms, Taylor gave in and left the room.

"I want Snagglepuss," she sobbed.

I chuckled. "I bet he will climb over you when you get home this afternoon and love you up."

I glanced down at Daisy's face. She was pale and had big dark bags under her eyes. The chemo had taken so much out of her, but this radiation was even worse. It tore my heart in two. I was so impressed by Taylor's strength; I wasn't sure I would be so calm if it were my kid.

"I like it when he climbs on me. I like his fatness on me; it's like a big blanket."

I chuckled. "He is fat because Daddy keeps sneaking him treats."

Daisy let out a small tired giggle. "He loves Snagglepuss and Titan."

I smiled. "I know he does. He pretends he doesn't, but he's a big softy underneath."

Daisy sighed and nodded her head. "I'm sleepy."

I kissed the top of Daisy's head. "Would you like me to put you into bed?"

Daisy shook her head. "No. I want to stay on your knee, but I want to sleep."

"Rest your head against my chest; you can sleep. I'll keep you safe."

Daisy placed her thumb in between her lips. "I believe you, Uncle Mav."

I smiled as she closed her eyes, and her breathing started to even out as she drifted into sleep. I would give my entire life to protect Daisy and her sister Imogen. I was never blessed with siblings or nephews and nieces. But these girls were most definitely my nieces. I would do anything in my power to keep them safe. Even if that meant giving up my life to do it. I would never understand those bastards that killed or hurt their kids. I looked down at Daisy again. Her long blonde eyelashes rested on her cheeks. At least she wouldn't lose her pretty blonde hair this time. Her blonde curls were only starting to get long again, and cupped her face.

Taylor stepped into the room and sighed. A smile crossed her lips as she saw Daisy asleep.

"I'm glad she's sleeping," Taylor whispered, handing me a takeaway coffee cup.

I smiled and reached for the coffee as I took a small sip. "She is missing Snagglepuss."

Taylor chuckled. "She and that cat are inseparable. Snagglepuss cries anytime he is locked away from her."

"He will always protect her."

Taylor smiled and nodded her head. "I'm glad. She has been through so much."

Taylor stared out at the window and sighed. "She has; you all have been," I said quietly."

"I keep asking God why. But I am starting to think God doesn't listen to me."

"I can't help you on that one. I don't believe in God."

Taylor turned to look at me and smiled. "I never did either. I actually read the bible when Daisy got sick. I even considered going to church. But every day, I watched my little girl get sicker and sicker, and God didn't seem to care."

Taylor's eyes welled with tears, and she sighed sadly. I didn't and would never understand if there was a god why he would hurt children and inflict them with diseases like cancer. Being a cop had killed any thought of religion in my mind. I'd seen the evillest of people working homicide. The things people did to one another were horrific, and the fact that this all-being entity refused to stop it didn't sit well with me.

Growing up, Dad sent me to a youth group run by the local church. The only thing I learned from that was not to go to the back room with the youth pastor because he liked to touch little boys. Obviously, one of the kids told me because the guy was arrested, and Dad pulled me out of there. He'd interrogated me, but thankfully I was smart enough to not trust anyone. Even as a seven-year-old, I didn't trust anyone. I wasn't sure if that was Dad's teaching or if it was ingrained in me. But either way, it had saved me from being molested as a kid and being more fucked up than I was. It probably also saved my father from being sent to prison. I guarantee if that sick bastard had touched me, Dad would have killed him.

"I bumped into the nurse outside before I came in; she said she is just waiting on the discharge paperwork, and then we will be able to take Daisy home."

I smiled and pressed a small kiss to the top of the little girl's head, feeling her blonde curls tickle my nose. "That's good; her bed will be far more comfortable to sleep in than on my chest."

Taylor chuckled. "Uncle Mav's chest is way more comforting."

"Her and Imogen have my chest anytime they need it."

"You're a good man Mav. I'm glad that we have you in our lives. I'm not sure I could have ever done this alone."

I smiled over at Taylor. "You, Harris, and the girls are family, which is what family does."

Chapter Nine

Killer

"There we go, Mr. Ryson," I said with a smile as I fluffed the pillows on the elderly man who watched me with keen eyes. He might have been old and frail, but his mind was sharp. Dementia hadn't touched him. I could see it in his eyes and how he watched me. He was a manipulator. I'd seen him plotting and scheming. I was never sure what he was planning, but I knew he was.

"Thank you, dear," he said wearily.

"Come on, let me get you back into bed; you look tired. Haven't you been sleeping?"

Mr. Ryson sighed and shrugged his shoulders. "I don't like it here. I'd rather be in my own bed."

"I understand. Why are you here, Mr. Ryson?" I questioned as I took the man by his elbow and helped him to the freshly made bed. He slipped between the sheets and shuffled down so his head was on the pillows.

"Selfishness and greed," he snorted. "I raised children to be just like me. Full of greed, always chasing the dollar, and look where it got me."

He sneered and shook his head before turning to the window. His eyes glazed and unfocused as he got lost in his thoughts.

"What did you do before you retired?"

"I was a lawyer, a Queen's counsel barrister. One of the highest-paid lawyers in Australia. I got some of the most feared men off of their charges. I was known as the bulldog of Melbourne." Mr. Ryson chuckled and shook his head. "I regret it, you know. I regret working so hard and not spending more time at home with my family. But you get what you give. And I gave fuck all to my family, so now I'm reaping what I sowed."

I sighed. "It's not right, though. You are still their father?"

Mr. Ryson shrugged his shoulders. "I was a pretty lousy father, if I'm honest. I was a workaholic and spent more time rubbing shoulders with the worst of the worse than I did at home raising my kids. I always hated that my father had the attitude that children should be seen and not heard, but I grew into him. Just as my sons have grown into me. I should be proud. They have taken over the law firm I built from the ground. They have taken over the work I did. The only difference is they were smart enough to inflict their selfishness onto children."

I smiled sadly and shook my head. I still felt it was unfair. It didn't matter that Mr. Ryson didn't spend time with his kids; he still put food in their bellies and a roof over their heads. The least they could do was not let the man rot away in a nursing home.

"Never mind, death will visit me one of these days soon, and I'll get some peace."

"Is that what you want?" I asked.

Mr. Ryson looked at me with narrowed eyes before he finally sighed. "Yeah. I'm not scared of death. I've met enough men that would kill me in a blink of an eye if they saw fit. Death isn't something I've ever feared."

"Do you believe in heaven and hell, Mr. Ryson?"

The older man snorted and shook his head. "Not at all. As a kid, I prayed too many times to stop my old man from whipping me, but he kept doing it. I soon realized that it was arrogant of me to think that there would be a god that would personally hear my prayer and decide to answer mine. In contrast, little ones were dying of cancer and awful diseases. No. I think we blink out."

I hummed. "I'd like to hope that paradise is waiting for me, that maybe I will see my mum again one day."

Mr. Ryson shrugged his shoulders. "I guess if you have someone that has already passed that you miss, it would be beneficial to believe in heaven. But I have no one on the other side I want to see again."

"Not even your wife?"

Mr. Ryson threw his head back and barked out a laugh. "Jesus, no. That bitch would probably try to kill me even in death. She hated me. I don't blame her. I was an asshole. You all look at me as some frail older man who needs aid. But I assure you, I wasn't always like that. I was once a philandering, womanizing bastard. I didn't give a fuck about anyone. And my missus knew it. She knew her place. She knew that the way she would survive our marriage was in silence. Don't kid yourself, dear; I was a cunt."

My eyes widened at the brutalness of Mr. Ryson's tone. I nodded my head and licked over my bottom lip.

"We'll have a good night, Mr. Ryson; I will return later to give you your medication."

He gave me a tight smile and a firm nod before he reached for his television remote and turned on the tv that hung over his bed. I sighed and walked out of the man's room. I had thought that there would be more time between my callings. But as I walked toward the medicine room, I knew it was time. Mr. Ryson needed to get his wish. It was time.

Chapter Ten

Nathan

"Detective Nathan Price," I answered as I continued to stare at the screen of my laptop.

"Hi, Nathan, it's Dean Richards calling."

"Oh, hey, Dean, how's it going? Harris said you were looking into some other old cases that could be related to our retirement killer."

"Catchy name," Dean chuckled, making me laugh. "Yeah, I was looking into the cases; I've found a few that had private carers, all women, and from the description, it all sounds like the same woman. I will email you the files and the next of kin. Hopefully, you can talk to them and see if it is the same person."

"Great, thank you," I replied as my email alerted me to Dean's email.

"That wasn't the only reason I was calling. I've been told we have a body coming in; this one is high profile. Does the name Arthur Ryson mean anything to you?"

My eyes widened, and I gasped. "As in the gangland barrister?"

"The one and only. He had been in a nursing home, Bartholomew Central in Sunshine. Apparently, he died under some strange circumstances. The nurse on duty was a new employee named Lisa Rizzo. Anyway, they suspect that Arthur was trying to climb out of bed and had a fall, but I'm suspicious; according to the other nursing staff, Arthur was spry; he might have been elderly and a bit frail, but he still had all his faculties and hadn't had any falls."

I hummed. "Interesting. Do we know anything about Lisa Rizzo?"

"Nothing that I know, but it wasn't my duty to ask, but I thought I might give you the heads up."

"Thanks, Dean," I said before ending the call and standing from my desk. The others were in the SKU room, poring over various files and information. I wish we could work one case at a time. Unfortunately, we didn't have that luxury. "Hey guys, Dean just called. Apparently, there was another suspicious death at a nursing home last night. This one was at Bartholomew Central, and the death was that of Arthur Ryson."

Harris's eyes widened, and his mouth dropped open. "Oh shit, that is going to make headlines."

I nodded my head. "It's possibly also going to make our job a little harder. But the nurse on duty was apparently a new nurse named Lisa Rizzo. They think that Arthur had a fall that killed him, but some other nurses are questioning it. I guess we will know more once Dean has had a chance to perform an autopsy."

"His death is going to open up a lot of potential suspects. It could be our retirement killer, but that man worked with many bad people. It could be fucking anyone," Landyn groaned.

I nodded. "I agree. Dean also emailed me the files of some patients that died suspiciously after having a private nurse. I've got the contacts of the next of kin. Let us contact them and take the photo of our mystery nurse to see if it is the same."

"I've been doing a bit of research into Sophie Haugh. I'm with James on this one," Charlee said. "It looks so much like her." Charlee turned the computer screen around, and on it was a picture of a woman dressed in all black. "That was taken twenty years ago at her mother's funeral. Obviously, in twenty years' time, people, but I could swear it's the same woman."

I hummed as I glanced at the photo we had taped to the wall. The resemblance was uncanny, but I couldn't be sure until we had proof that they were the same people.

"What are the odds that a child of a famous movie star would become a mass murderer?" Paola mused.

"That's what I'm not getting," Charlee answered. "I mean, she has left everything in her mother's will. I've learned that she has three mansions, a car collection, and so much money she doesn't have to work a day. Why go and become an underpaid nurse?"

I nodded. It wasn't adding up. I breathed in and slowly let it out. "Keep seeing what you can find. See if you can find out where Sophie perhaps lives. That might give us a better idea if this is the same woman. Maybe it is just someone with an uncanny likeness. In the meantime, I will contact the next of kin for the private patients Dean sent me and organize to talk to them. Hopefully, they will be able to recognize our nurse, and maybe they will know her real name. Have you run the other names through the system?"

Landyn nodded. "Yeah, nothing. I think they are all fake; nothing has come up, no birth or death certificates."

"That's what I thought might be the case. If you are going to go and murder people at your job, you probably are stupid if you use a real name."

Landyn smirked. "There are some pretty dumb people out there."

I chuckled and nodded before heading back to my computer to review the files Dean had sent me.

Chapter Eleven

Harris

"Daddy," Imogen screeched as I walked through the front door with a chuckle. I would never get sick of being greeted with such enthusiasm. I lifted my daughter and held her close, peppering her face with kisses.

"How's my big girl? What did you do at school today?" I asked as I carried her through the living room, where Daisy was lying on the couch beside Maverick. Her eyes were closed, and I noticed the heavy dark bags on her cheeks. My heart tore a little more. It had been a hell of a day, and I was glad she was resting.

"It was okay. But Jayden Parker hit me," Imogen growled.

I turned and looked at her with a frown. "Is that the same boy that keeps pulling your hair?"

Imogen nodded her head. "I hate him. I told him that you are a policeman with Uncle Maverick and that hitting people was against the law."

"That's right; what did he say?"

"He hit me again and said a bad word about you."

My eyes widened, and I looked at Mav, who appeared just as thunderous. "What word did he say?"

Imogen giggled. "I can't say it because I'll get in trouble."

"I give you a pass this one time."

Imogen looked over at her mother, who was watching Imogen with a smirk on her lips. "Can I say it, Mum?"

"Just this one time," Taylor repeated.

Imogen nodded her head. "He said that all cops are fat cunts and that you wouldn't be able to catch him."

Maverick choked on the air, and I cleared my throat. I wasn't sure what I had expected to come out of my daughter's mouth, but that was certainly not it.

"Well, it certainly isn't a nice boy, is he?" I growled. "I think maybe I'm going to have to go and have a chat with your teacher. No one should be allowed to hit you. Did you tell Mrs. Lane?"

Imogen nodded her head and sighed. "Yeah, but she doesn't care. Jayden never gets in trouble. She says, stay away from him. But I do stay away from him. But then he comes looking for me just to be annoying."

My frown deepened. That was predatory behavior, and if it wasn't nipped in the bud soon, I would see that kid one day on the news. I hated the whole boys hit girls who they like. No one should be fucking hitting anyone.

"Alright, I'm going to go and speak to Mrs. Lane tomorrow."

"And I'm going to go and speak to Jayden's father," Maverick growled, making me smirk. If there was a man that was even more protective of my girls than me, it was their big scary Uncle Maverick.

"Can I just stay home? I can help look after Daisy?" Imogen whined. Jayden's actions had to be affecting her; that girl loved school. There was no way that she would want to stay home.

"I'm afraid not, little miss; you have to go to school so you can be as smart as your mum one day," I replied before kissing the top of her hair. "But for now, how about you come in the kitchen with me, and we can make a start on dinner."

Imogen huffed, but as I put her down, she slipped her little hand into mine and escorted me to the kitchen. My mind was racing; I wouldn't say I liked the idea that my daughter was being bullied; tomorrow morning, I would go and speak to her teacher and find out exactly why she hadn't done anything to stop it. I know that teachers are overworked, but damn, if you can't even prevent physical bullying, that is a problem.

"Right, what are we going to cook?"

Imogen tapped on her chin and hummed as I swung the door to the refrigerator open and stared at the contents. There wasn't much in there; I was going to have to go and do some grocery shopping. I thought about what to do: I could dash out to the shops or organize a delivery for tomorrow morning.

A chirp sounded behind me, and when I turned, my eyes widened as I noticed not only Snagglepuss and Titan but Thor was also there.

"Maverick, what is your cat doing here?" I growled.

I heard Maverick's cackle before his footsteps sounded, and he appeared in the kitchen. "I couldn't leave Thor at home by himself. Besides, he loves the girls and their kittens."

I rolled my eyes. "This place is going to be turned into a zoo."

"Hardly," Maverick snorted. "Come on, let me order us all some pizza, and then you can do an order for some groceries."

I yawned as I nodded my head. As much as I didn't think much of cats, I was glad that the girls had one each, I'd seen how much Snagglepuss loved Daisy, and I couldn't ask for a better therapy animal. Even if the fucking thing shit in my shoes when he was in a bad mood with me.

Chapter Twelve

Maverick

Fuming was an understatement; even livid was too soft of a word for what I felt. It turns out that this little prick Jayden had been bullying Imogen for the last year. At first, it had just been name-calling and stuff that was easy to ignore, but now it had become physical. When Taylor gave Imogen a bath last night, she noticed bruises on Imogen's back and arms and found out the bruises were caused by the little bastard hitting her.

I was ropable, and there was no way that Harris would go and sweet talk a teacher. The teacher was just as guilty of that cunts behavior as his parents were. I'd already texted Nathan to see if Jayden's father was on our books. And what do you know, of course, he was. Domestic violence 101. Jayden was learning from the best, and if it wasn't curbed now, the kid would end up the same as his old man.

"You know you didn't have to come," Harris said as we climbed out of the car and flanked Imogen.

"Yes, I did," I said as I glared around the school playground, looking for any kid that wanted to cause my niece problems. I'd break their fucking fingers.

"You are scaring the kids," Harris whispered with a chuckle.

"Good, then they will know Imogen isn't to be messed with."

Harris snorted and rolled his eyes. "I swear you are a menace."

I grinned and nodded as a little girl called Imogen's name. The girl with dark skin and braids in her hair came running toward us and opened her arms to give Imogen a hug.

"Hey, is this your uncle Maverick?" the little girl asked, looking up at me with wide eyes.

I could have sworn Imogen puffed her chest out as much as I did when I realized she'd been talking about me.

"Yep, he and Dad are here to speak to Mrs. Lane about Jayden."

The girl's eyes widened, and a huge grin spread across her lips. "Good. Maybe they will finally kick Jayden out of school."

"Does he hit you too?" I asked with a frown pulling at my brow.

"He has, but my brother punched him back, and he hasn't hit me since."

I smirked. "It's great to have a big brother who will protect you."

The girl grinned and bounced her head up and down. "Yep. I asked him to look after Imogen, but Jayden hits her when I'm not around, so I don't see it."

"Okay, well, we will ensure it doesn't happen anymore to anyone. Does Jayden only hit girls?"

"Yep," Imogen answered. "He is scared of the boys."

"Typical," I heard Harris mutter. It was typical abuser behavior. They always targeted those that were younger, more minor, or more easily manipulated. They never went after those who could and would fight back. That wouldn't be an easy battle to win.

"Okay, well, while you two go off to play, Mav and I will go and speak with Mrs. Lane," Harris said before leaning down and kissing Imogen. Imogen wrapped her arms around my waist, and I kissed her blonde hair before waving her off as she ran beside her friend, chatting wildly.

"I'm glad she's got a good friend."

"Yeah, that's Violet. She is a great kid and comes from a fantastic family. Her older brother is a year above them and has always been super protective of Violet and Imogen. Still, as she said, this kid targets them when Violet isn't around."

I sighed and nodded my head. We moved toward the front office building and stepped into the stuffy, overheated hallway before walking down toward the room where Imogen had her class. Knocking on the door, we drew the attention of a short, fat woman with so much makeup on her face that she looked like she might have applied it with a spatula.

"Mrs. Lane?" I said gruffly.

"Yes, but it's Miss now," she purred as she looked me up and down. My top lip curled over my teeth in a sneer. I hated women like this. They had a fucking job to do that didn't include hitting on possible parents of students.

"I'm Detective Maverick Wolfe; this is my partner Detective Harris Bishop." The teacher's eyes flared before she quickly schooled her face.

"What can I do for you?" she asked, clearing her throat.

"Well, for one, you can stop that little animal, Jayden Parker, from hitting my niece, Imogen Bishop. You didn't even tell him off, especially when she came to you for help. Imogen is covered in bruises from that boy's mistreatment."

Miss. Lane licked nervously over her bottom lip. "Is this police business."

"It will be if he continues to assault Imogen."

"Oh. Um. The problem is that Jayden comes from a very violent home, and we don't like to ring his parents because we know that things will be bad for him."

I folded my arms across my chest and raised my brow. "You are a mandated reporter, no?"

"Yes."

"And have you reported Jayden's homelife?"

"Well, no, because I haven't seen any evidence of abuse on Jayden."

"So, you're telling me that this boy comes from a violent home, and you know it's a violent home, but he's never come to school with bruises?"

"He has sometimes but usually says he bumped into something."

I shook my head and sneered. "What you're saying is that you have seen evidence of abuse on this child and have ignored it because you're too fucking lazy to do your job."

Miss. Lane's eyes widened, and she gasped. "No, no, that's not it," she argued vehemently as she shook her head. "I just don't have a lot of time."

"You think that boy deserves to live in such a horrible home?"

"No, of course not," she shrieked.

"They you would find the time to contact children's services. In the meantime, if I see one more bruise on my niece or if she comes home and tells me that this boy has been picking on her again, it will become a police matter, and I will be coming after you as well. Are we clear?"

Miss Lane cleared her throat and nodded her head. "Yes, we are clear. I'll make sure that he isn't anywhere near Imogen."

"And ring children's services; that kid needs help, and it's your job to help them."

I turned and stormed out of the classroom with Harris behind me. Once we were outside the building, Harris began to chuckle.

"I didn't even say a word."

I snorted. "No one picks on my nieces and gets away with it," I growled. I'd made a promise the minute that Imogen and Daisy were born. If anything happened to Harris, I would take on that father role for them. But I would also protect them with my life, even with Harris. They might not share my DNA, but I wouldn't let them ever get hurt.

Chapter Thirteen

Nathan Harris looked like he had much on his mind as he entered the office. I couldn't imagine what it would be like to have a child that was so sick. My heart ached for him and his family. I wished I could do more, but unfortunately, this wasn't a problem I could fix. They were the worst kind of problems. I had become a cop because I liked fixing problems. I was always the diplomat of the family. If my sisters were fighting, they always approached me to discuss it. But in Daisy's case, there was no fixing it. Cancer was a bitch of a disease, and it always broke my heart when I saw kids suffering.

"Hey man, I have that file for you."

Harris looked at me with confusion etched on his face. "File?"

I nodded. "Maverick asked me to pull a file on Dwayne Parker."

Harris chuckled and rolled his eyes. "Maverick is like a dog with a fucking bone. My daughter Imogen has been getting bullied at school by a boy. Maverick had ideas of going to the father and reading him the riot act."

I winced. "Yeah, if you can talk him out of that, it might be a good idea. This guy isn't an angel by any means."

"I figured as much. What's he done for?"

"One hundred and fifty-seven arrests for domestic violence, and not once sent to prison. Even his possession charges were miraculously dropped."

Harris stared at me with wide eyes. "Seriously? Is he a fucking politician, son, or something?"

I shrugged my shoulders. "No idea, but it has to be something to get away with it for so long."

"Yeah. Anyway, thanks, man. Where are we on the retirement killer?"

I moved over to my desk and lifted the folder that Dean had dropped in. "This is Arthur Ryson," I explained as I held up the folder. "He was at Bartholomew Central. Appeared healthy and fit, with no signs of dementia, but was starting to take falls, so his family placed him in the home. Yesterday morning, he was found dead on the floor of his room by the morning shift nurse. At first, they had assumed he'd fallen while getting up. Apparently, he was a pretty independent guy."

Harris nodded. "Yeah, I remember him as a barrister; he got a lot of very nasty men out of jail."

I nodded. "Yeah, I've been looking into the cases; I had wondered at first if this was the retirement killer or could be someone who had a beef with him and decided to get revenge while he was at his most frail."

"What were you about to find out?"

"Dean's report said that Arthur had blunt force trauma to the front of his head, consistent with a fall. They were able to find blood on the edge of a cabinet. However, his bloodwork tells me we are looking at the retirement killer. He had large quantities of insulin in his system. Dean believes the insulin wasn't enough to kill him immediately but make him feel sick. He felt that Arthur tried to get out of bed to either the bathroom or to get a nurse but either stumbled and hit his head or collapsed."

"So, was it the insulin or the fall that killed him?"

"Hard to say. Dean said that both could have been fatal."

Harris hummed. "Is the first suspicious death we have had from Bartholomew Central?"

I nodded. "Yep."

"And have they taken on any new staff?"

"They have," Charlee said from behind us. "I've just got off the phone to the director there. Apparently, they had one new nurse, orderly and maintenance guy start in the last two weeks."

"Okay, so that might help us to narrow down our culprit. Did any of the three disappear this morning?" I asked.

Charlee shook her head. "None that have been reported as missing. The nurse was working the night shift on Arthur's ward last night."

"What is her name?" I asked.

Charlee glanced down at her notepad. "Lisa Rizzo. The director, Madeline, is sending over Lisa's file along with the other two new staff members."

"Great, as soon as that arrives, we will have an address for Lisa; I think she needs to be looked into further."

"Agreed; Madeline said she would send the files through now, so I'll check my emails."

"Thanks, Charlee," I replied before turning back to Harris. "If your little girl needs help with her bully, just ask; I'm with Maverick."

Harris smiled. "You remind me so much of him. Are you sure you two aren't related?"

I snorted and shook my head. "My family is big, but not big enough to miss a whole branch."

Chapter Fourteen

Killer

"Ms. Rizzo, please come in," the nursing director Madeline McKormick called as I rapped my knuckles lightly on the door. I gave her a tight smile and a nod as I crossed the threshold to see two men who I knew had to be cops sitting in the office.

My heart was pounding, and I could hear the blood rushing in my ears.

"Take a seat," Madeline directed and paused while I sat beside the younger man opposite the director. "Lisa, these are Detectives Nathan Price and Harris Bishop; they have questions about Mr. Ryson's death last night and were made aware that you were his night nurse."

I nodded and licked nervously over my bottom lip. I sucked in a deep breath before facing the two cops.

"I did it," I exclaimed.

The younger cop blinked and stared at me with confusion while the older one smirked as if he already knew.

"You did what exactly, Lisa?" Madeline asked.

I sighed and shook my head. "I killed Mr. Ryson. And my name isn't Lisa. It is Sophie. Sophie Haugh. I'm responsible for Mr. Ryson's death and many others."

"Oh my god," Madeline gasped.

The older cop stood with a firm nod. "Then I think it would be best for you to escort us to the police station to discuss this further and on record."

I nodded but said nothing else. I stood and stared at the two detectives who took me gently by the arms. "I am not going to cuff you. Are you going to give me any trouble?" the older cop asked.

"No," I replied with another sigh. Heat crept into my cheeks at the thought of everyone seeing me handcuffed and being frog-marched out of the building. Not that anyone really knew who I was.

I'd not planned on confessing, but I guess it was time. I felt wrong about Mr. Ryson's death; he hadn't gone smoothly and fought me. In the back of my mind, I knew that this would be the last time I did Death's work. I wasn't a reaper of souls anymore. Now I was simply a murderer.

"We will speak to you again soon, Madeline," the younger cop said as they escorted me out of the office.

We walked silently through the quiet halls; nurses and patients seemed to stare wonderfully at us as we passed them. I was sure I could hear the walls whispering, telling everyone in the building that I had handled the death of Arthur Ryson. When we found him on the floor, I thought I might get away with it, that perhaps the coroner would rule it as a fall. But I was stupid.

On the ride to the police station, I didn't say a word. The police didn't ask me any questions, and I didn't offer any information. There was time for that, and I wouldn't say I liked repeating myself. Mother had always taught me there was no point in talking for the sake of talking.

"Only speak when you have something intelligent and worthy to say. Otherwise, you will look like a fool," she would instruct when I would fill her ears with chatter about the most inane things.

As a child, I didn't understand the power of words and how humans spoke too often. Once I learned to be quiet and listen more than I said, it was surprising how much I picked up. All sorts of information from our neighbors who were sleeping around on each other and pretending they didn't. This milkman had been arrested for touching Nigel Robertson at number sixteen.

Nigel's father had shouted long into the night about how he planned to kill the milkman. Mother said that she'd never trusted the milkman, Dennis Lawson. She said he always gave her a strange feeling. A feeling that she was right about. Dennis Lawson was found hung from a tree at Camberwell station only days later.

Of course, the rumor was that Nigel's father had done it, but no one was ever arrested. However, it was a story that would stick in my mind for a long time. As I grew, I wondered much about Dennis Lawson and whether he was sent to hell. If I believed the preachers at our Sunday school growing up, I would have believed that God forgave Dennis before he died. But I preferred to think that somewhere Dennis was judged harshly and not living in paradise.

Then again, murder was a sin; I wondered if that meant when the day I died came if I too would end up in hell. But then again, was I really murdering people? I mean, those people that I killed were tired and wanted to die. They might not have said it out loud, but I heard it in the way they looked at me and the way that they reminisced about the past. Or in the way that they got so lost that they forgot they were now in their eighties, rotting away in a nursing home while some nurse wiped their ass for them.

All except Arthur Ryson. I shouldn't have killed him. But I couldn't have stopped myself if I tried. And maybe it will be for his death that I end up in hell. Like Nigel's father, I was righting a wrong, but perhaps it was me who was wrong.

Chapter Fifteen

Nathan

When we walked into the office at Bartholomew Central, I hadn't expected that we would walk out with a woman who confessed she was a serial killer. Let alone a woman who was the daughter of an actress and appeared to be at least seventy years old.

Madeline had confirmed that our suspected killer was the same woman working for her but under the name of Lisa Rizzo. I wasn't sure how deep her crimes went or how many victims she had, but I was curious to learn more. Mostly I wanted to know why?

"Well, shit, which wasn't what I was expecting," Harris said as he leaned against the wall after we had placed Sophie into an interview room.

"I'm shocked," I replied. "I mean, she just blurted it out."

Harris hummed and nodded his head. "Let's go and gather up all of the files so we can discover just how many people she has actually killed."

I followed Harris down the hall and into the SKU room. "I heard you arrested someone," Charlee said as I entered the room.

"Yeah, Sophie Haugh."

Charlee's eyes widened, and her mouth dropped open. "As in Lucille Haugh's daughter."

I nodded. "Appears to be. And she confessed to at least Arthur Ryson's murder."

"Seriously?"

I nodded again. "We will take the files to the interview room and see if she will confess to the others."

"She might just be tired of doing this. I wonder why she did it at all."

"That's what I'm curious about too. I don't know if this is like some Angel of Death or if she just thirsts for killing."

Charlee hummed and leaned back in her seat. "Hopefully, she cops on all her murders; then it will be an easy wrap-up. This one I'm working on now, I could really do with some help, so it would be great to have some extras."

"Cold case?"

Charlee nodded. "Yeah, all indigenous teenage girls, killed between eighty-one and eighty-seven, dumped on the highways, raped, beaten, and their throats cut."

"And no other ones after eighty-seven?"

"Not that I can find, but I've sent out for other precincts across Australia to see if maybe there are more in other states."

"Were all of the bodies dumped in Melbourne?"

"Yeah, that's what strikes me as weird. I know that now, Melbourne is a bit of a multicultural melting pot, but back in the eighties, it was still pretty heavily white; the indigenous that did live here blended in, like this killer had to be specifically seeking out the girls."

I frowned and scratched at my chin as I thought about it. It wasn't until 1966 that the white policy in Australia ended. At that time, the government finally recognized Indigenous people as humans; before that, they were classed as fauna. Which, in my mind, is totally disgusting. But even twenty years later, Melbourne hadn't a huge Indigenous population. Charlee was right. This killer had to have sought out the girls for them to be all Indigenous.

"All of the girls were black?" I asked.

"Yep."

I hummed again. That was weird. Today, in Melbourne, in particular, we have a large population of Indigenous people, many of whom have fair skin. They didn't fit the stereotypical look of the Indigenous.

"Once we've got this case caught up, I'll be able to help you. It's certainly a strange one."

"You're telling me. I'm completely stumped. And worse is that no DNA was kept from any of the rape kits."

I sighed and shook my head. "That actually rings true. Although the Indigenous garnered rights by the eighties, there were still a lot of people that saw them as animals or savages. If the cops working the case didn't think it mattered that Indigenous girls were targeted, they wouldn't have investigated too much."

Charlee nodded. "Yeah, I gathered as much. The notes are minimal at best. I'm starting to wonder if other girls are out there and were never even reported on."

"I hate that our country was so racist for so long."

"A problem that still exists today."

"Yeah, you're right, thankfully not as bad as back then. Were all the girls found?"

"Yes, that was the one good thing. Apparently, every girl was reported missing before their bodies were discovered."

"That's a start; it will at least give us more details about the girls and where they were likely taken from. Then we can focus on those areas. You should contact the families; maybe they will have thought of some more information since the deaths."

"Good idea."

I smiled and turned to the doorway where Harris murmured with Derek. I could see the strain on Harris's face and gathered he must have been discussing his daughter. I really wish that I'd been able to give Harris my holidays. He needed to be home with his family, not working a damned case.

Sighing, I walked over to the two men. Harris smiled as I approached. "Ready to see how many others she killed?"

"Definitely," I replied, smiling before turning away and heading for the interview room where we'd left Sophie Haugh.

Chapter Sixteen

Harris

I had gathered all the files we'd accumulated for this case as Nathan talked to Charlee about an issue she was working on. From the snippets I could hear, I knew that we would be helping her with that case next.

"How's the boy doing?" Derek asked as he came up behind me.

I chuckled. "He's hardly a boy."

Derek snorted. "He is to me."

I grinned and nodded. There was no denying we were getting older. Derek wasn't much older than me, but still probably old enough to be Nathan's father. "He's doing really well. Have you earmarked him?"

Derek smiled slyly. "I have. I see something in him. Very similar to what I saw in you and Maverick."

I nodded. "Yep, he reminds me of Maverick when I first met him. Fuck, even now, Mav hasn't really changed."

"He is a great cop. His Dad would have been very proud of the man he raised."

I sighed and nodded. "Yeah, he would have been."

I only had a chance to get to know Maverick's father briefly before he passed away, but what I learned of the man was that he was a perfect cop. Maverick did everything he could to emulate that.

"How are you doing?"

I sighed again. "I'm alright. I must admit, I hate being here instead of at home with my girl."

"Yeah, I get that. I wish there was something I could have done."

I shrugged my shoulders. "Daisy is enjoying having Uncle Mav and Thor at the house."

Derek's eyes widened. "You let him bring the cat?"

I barked out a laugh and shook my head. "No. I got home from work, and there the damned thing was, the king of the castle with his two servants. I would have told him to take the cat home, but it seems I can never say no to the kids or him."

Derek laughed loudly. "That is where your girls learn their best puppy dog eyes."

I chuckled and nodded. It wouldn't have surprised me. Maverick was a bad influence on those girls. He spoiled them rotten, and I wouldn't have it any other way. Nathan came to where I was standing.

"Ready?"

"Yep," he replied with a grin, and we walked away from Derek and toward the interview room where our confessed killer was sitting. I wondered if she was guilty of all the crimes we had on the books or just Mr. Ryson's.

Swinging open the door, Sophie sat on one of the cold metal chairs with her elbows on the table in front of her and her face in her hands. When she looked up at us coming in through the door, I could see her eyes were red from crying.

"Hi Sophie, how are you doing? Do you need a drink or to use the bathroom before we start?" Nathan asked.

Sophie shook her head. "No. I want to get all of this over and done with."

"Okay, well, there are a few things we need to go through first before we can start," Nathan explained as we took our seats on the other side of the table. "Firstly, I must let you know that this conversation is recorded." Nathan pointed to the camera that sat in the corner of the room. Sophie glanced up at the camera before nodding her head. "You don't have to speak to us; you can stop speaking to us anytime. You can also have legal representation before and while speaking to us. You can ask for legal representation at any time during the interview, and the conversation will halt until your lawyer arrives. Do you understand all of that, Sophie?"

"Yeah," she replied with a sigh. "I want to talk to you. I don't need a lawyer; I admit I'm guilty."

Nathan smiled and nodded his head. He opened the file on top, which was Mr. Ryson's. "You said in Madeline McKormick's office that you were guilty of killing Mr. Ryson. Can we begin by talking about that?"

Sophie shrugged her shoulders. "He wasn't supposed to be one of the ones I saved, but I went against the plan. That's why I'm here."

Nathan frowned and glanced at me. "Can you explain that to me?"

Chapter Seventeen

Sophie

"What do you want to know?" I asked. My head felt like it was screaming at me to not say anything, but what was the point. I'd been caught. I'd got greedy and killed someone that wasn't mine to kill.

"Well, you said you killed Mr. Ryson; what did you do?" the cop, who'd introduced himself as Nathan, asked. I looked over at him. If I were younger, I would have fallen for a man that looked like him.

Who am I kidding? There was no way I could have ever fallen for anyone; Mother took up all my time. It was why I'd never married or had children of my own. It wasn't out of not wanting it. God, how much I'd wanted to have a child. But I was busy looking after Mother.

I breathed deeply and slowly let it out before running my hand over my face. "Maybe we need to begin with the start; I can probably think more clearly then."

"Sure," Nathan replied.

"When I was twenty-five years old, my mother took ill. She became severely depressed; we couldn't get her out of bed, and she no longer wanted to do anything she once did. I had to basically force-feed her. I don't know if she wanted to die or was just sad at the hand life had dealt her, but her idea was to stay in bed and waste away. I became her career. I did everything for her, from washing to feeding and cleaning the house. Mother was a very private woman, the press had given her grief over the years while she was on television, and she wanted nothing more to do with it. So, she stayed in bed, and I did everything for her. Then when I was forty-three, she finally passed away."

"Sophie, were you responsible for your mother's death?"

I smiled at the older cop, Harris. I could see why he would ask that. I shook my head. "No. By the time she died, she had dementia and, most days, had no idea what was up or down. I watched my mother literally fade away and be replaced by a shell. Just a body. Until one day, she didn't wake up. After she died and we had her funeral. The media forgot about me again, so I decided to take up nursing. I applied to universities, but I couldn't get into any of the universities because I'd been home-schooled with no reliable education. So, I worked out how to lie. I fabricated my credentials and my certificates and started to apply for jobs. At first, I worked as a private nurse; I thought it would be less obvious that I wasn't qualified than if I worked in a nursing home."

Harris flipped open the file in front of him. "Did you use the name Sophie Haugh there?"

I shook my head. "No. I went by the name Janelle Olson. I don't know where I came up with the name; it just came to me one day. Anyway, I spent four years being a private nurse for four patients."

"And did you kill any of them?" Nathan asked, making me chuckle.

"No, I didn't. They died, but they all died not by my hand. Mr. Alexander had cancer and passed away at ninety-seven, Ingrid Bertram had dementia, and she passed at eighty-eight; Margaret Davis was ninety-four and died as a result of a stroke she'd had previously to me starting. Jim Bruce also had dementia. He was one hundred and four, if you can believe it. But it was them that made me realize. I realized that these people were wasting away. They, like my mother, were nothing but a shell. They weren't living; they were waiting to die. I watched as Jim's son put his father's dog to sleep because he felt it was cruel to keep the dog alive, but he hired a private nurse to try and extend his father's life. I mean, the man was one hundred and four. It was cruel."

I breathed in and let out a slow exhale. "After Jim died, I applied to work at Whispering Willows. I changed my name, falsified my references, and did a few other things, but I knew what to do. I had a calling."

"A calling?" Nathan asked with wide eyes.

I nodded my head. "I was an angel for death. I realized that maybe death had so many other lives to take because of the wars and everything going on that he didn't have time to get to these people and therefore needed other humans to help him. When I started working at Whispering Willows, I saw my opportunity. I researched what would be the easiest way to kill someone. I didn't want to be cruel; I didn't want to prolong their death. And I only ever euthanized those that were in too much pain or that were just shells. Those ravaged by dementia, the ones that no longer knew who their loved ones were, or who they were."

Nathan's frown was pulled hard on his brow as he looked at me. "Sophie, how many people do you think you've murdered?"

I shrugged my shoulders. "There has to be at least twenty-seven."

"Christ," Harris whispered. "I'm going to get a piece of paper and would like you to write down as many as you can remember for me."

I nodded and watched as Harris left the room. "I wasn't trying to be malicious to these people or their families. I never took from them financially; I never stole anything from them. I just wanted to bring them peace."

"Sophie," Nathan said as his eyes bored into mine. "I believe you."

Chapter Eighteen

Harris

Jesus Christ. I didn't even know what to think about this. "Fuck, I would never have guessed that sweet-looking old lady was responsible for twenty-seven fucking deaths," Maverick said as I exited the interview room.

"Me neither," I chuckled with a shake of my head. "What are you doing here?"

"Taylor and the girls were going to have a spa day and watch a movie, so I thought I'd leave them to it."

"You didn't want a pedicure and your toenails painted?"

Maverick's lips broke into a wide grin. "Who said I didn't stay for the pedicure? I have gorgeous purple toenails now."

I threw my head back with a laugh. "Oh man, you are the best uncle."

Maverick's grin grew impossibly wider, and his chest puffed with pride. I quickly reached out and pulled my best friend into my arms in a tight embrace. "Thank you, Mav, for everything."

Maverick patted my back and looked into my eyes. "I love you like a brother, and those two little girls are my nieces; I will do everything I can to take some of the pressure off you and Taylor. You have both been dealt a rough hand, and I won't sit idly by when I know just getting to paint my toenails purple will put smiles on those little girls' faces."

I smiled and blinked hard to hold back the tears threatening to spill. I swallowed thickly, my tongue trapped with all the sappy shit I wanted to yell. Maverick seemed to understand as he gave me a wry grin.

"Get in there and discover how diabolic this old bitch is."

I snorted and stepped away from my partner before entering the interview room where Nathan was sitting with the folders on the tables. They had photos of the suspected deaths, and Sophie was going through each of them.

"That is all of them," she said as I sat at the desk.

"That's a total of thirty-four," Nathan explained.

"You only said twenty-seven earlier."

Sophie sighed and shrugged her shoulders. "I'd obviously forgotten some, but I could remember once Nathan showed me the pictures."

I nodded my head. "Alright. Sophie, you will be arrested for the murder of the thirty-four that you have shown. We will have the statement you gave us printed and ready for you to sign. The crown prosecutor, Monica Lewis, will speak with you in a little while. Then you will probably be taken to the Dame Phyllis Frost Center until you go before the judge. All of that will probably take some time before we can get you over there, so you can either stay in here or we can take you down to the cells where there is a bed and a bathroom. Nothing fancy, but it will be much more comfortable there than here."

"Yes, okay, I'd like to go to the cells. When will I be able to contact my lawyer?"

"We can get you to a phone once we get down to the cells if you like. Do you have his number?"

Sophie nodded her head. "I always committed it to memory; I knew I would probably need it one day."

I gave Sophie a tight smile before I stood. "Just hang tight here for a moment, and I'll organize someone to take you."

"Thank you," she replied as if I was some concierge that had just told her she would be shown to her hotel room.

Nathan gathered the files, and I went to the little office between the interview room. Pressing on the file for the interview video, I moved it over to the computer that would translate the entire transcript into a written document for Sophie to sign. It was so much easier with the advances in technology.

"Man, I can't believe that a sixty-four-year-old woman can be the murderer of thirty-four people," Nathan said with disbelief as he leaned against the doorway.

I glanced up and nodded my head. "Yeah, it is certainly a first for me. I would never have thought that was who we were looking for. It's rare enough to have a female serial killer, but to have one of her age that I've never seen."

"Charlee is working on a case that will probably need all of us on it after we hand this over to Monica."

"Yeah?" I asked, glancing up from the printed sheets of transcripts. "What is it?"

"A cold case from the eighties, all teenage girls, all Indigenous, raped and their throats cut before being left along highways."

"Indigenous?" I asked with a frown.

"Yep, and all from Melbourne."

"That's even rarer."

"That was what I was thinking. It's really stumped me."

I hummed and nodded my head. "Once we have Sophie's case sorted and sent to Monica, we will sit down with Charlee and see what she has. That one sounds like it's going to be a really tricky one. Especially if the guy has never been caught. It's rare enough to be killing teenage girls and leaving them on the highway, but for all of the girls to be Indigenous is even stranger."

Nathan nodded and stretched his arms above his head while yawning. "I am looking forward to bed tonight."

"Didn't sleep well?"

Nathan shook his head. "Nah," he answered but didn't elaborate. From the look on his face, I could tell that it wasn't work that had kept him up. I wondered if it was perhaps a partner, but then I wasn't sure if Nathan was single or attached. Hell, I didn't even know if he liked men or women. I suddenly realized that I knew very little about the guy. Any of them, really. Other than Maverick, I didn't know any of my colleagues. I felt guilty for being so consumed in my life that I hadn't stopped thinking that others had stuff going on for them too.

"Anything you want to talk about?"

Nathan smiled and shook his head again. "Nothing right now, but thank you, Harris; I will let you in once we are done."

I smiled and nodded before leaving the office to get Sophie to review and sign the transcripts.

Chapter Nineteen

Nathan

"Guys, you did an amazing job and so fast," Monica said as she entered the office.

"It was all our guy, Nathan," Maverick announced with a grand gesture to me, making me chuckle.

Monica grinned. "I can't believe that sweet little old lady down in booking is a mass murderer. Thirty-four deaths connected to her. It's unreal."

"She really thought she was helping them," I said.

Monica nodded her head. "I believe that too. She knows what she was doing was illegal and wrong, but at the same time, she felt she was doing them an honor by euthanizing them."

My phone started to buzz, and I glanced at the screen to see that it was my sister Thalia calling. I pressed the phone to my ear and left the office. "Hey, Tails, what's up?"

"It's Mum; she got out again."

"Shit," I groaned. "That's the fourth time in two weeks. How long was she gone for this time?"

"Four hours."

My eyes widened, and I gasped. "Are you serious? Why didn't you ring me?"

"Dad didn't want to bother you."

"Jesus, Tails, I'm a cop. I could have had the whole force out looking for her."

"I think if he hadn't found her at the playground, he was about to ring you, but don't be surprised if you hear about an old lady swinging on the swings at the playground with her legs in the air and no underwear on."

I groaned and rubbed my hand down over my face. "She's getting worse, Thalia."

"I know. Look, Nathan, we promised we wouldn't put her in a home, but we must revisit the idea."

I wanted to argue, but I couldn't. I thought about Sophie. She wasn't wrong; dementia and Alzheimer's was a fucking awful ailment. It destroyed the person and broke them down until they were nothing more than skin and bones. Their brains were nothing but a mass of holes. Tears burned at the thought of going against Mum's wishes. She'd been so set in her ways. She wanted to die in her home.

I scrubbed my hand down over my face. "Nathan?" Thalia said, reminding me that I hadn't answered her.

I cleared my throat. "We'll talk to Dad about it. I don't see him agreeing, though."

"I know, but he has to think clearly, Nath; he is aging too, and he can't keep a constant eye on her. He was napping when she escaped; he thought she was napping too. He feels horrible, and I can see the guilt eating him. I think he wouldn't ring you because he was scared that if the police got involved, it would show him he failed."

"Shit, Tails, he's not a failure. I couldn't do half of what he does with Mum."

"Me neither. The only other choice is for us to give up working full-time to help look after her. I'm the only one that doesn't have an important job, so I guess it would have to be me."

"No, Thalia. You can't do that. You and Henry are trying for a baby; you need all the money you can get."

Thalia sighed. I could hear the stress in her voice, which wouldn't help her body. Thalia and her husband Henry had been struggling to get pregnant for the last year. They'd been doing IVF, but so far, everything had failed. They'd even considered adoption, but even that had a long waiting list. I felt awful for her and wished there was something I could do. My sisters had all offered to surrogate for her, which I think they were considering. However, even if they did use a surrogate, they would still need stable housing and money for the baby. I wouldn't let her give up her work.

Thalia worked as a barista. It may not have been a job she needed to go to uni, but she was great at it, and the hospitality industry was built for her. I couldn't imagine her doing anything else.

"Look, I'll come round to Dad's tonight, and we can talk it out then."

"Okay," Thalia said quietly, but I could hear in her voice that she was preparing to give up everything. I would fight her to prevent it from happening. I would sooner give up my job to help than Thalia.

I wasn't married; I wasn't attached. I had no dependents and could always return to police work. The thought of leaving stung, but I would do whatever I had to do.

"Hey man, is everything alright?" I glanced up to see Maverick standing in the doorway.

I sighed and shook my head. "No. Nothing is alright."

Maverick stepped out of the doorway and wrapped his arm around my shoulders. "Come on, let's go and grab a coffee and have a chat."

I nodded. I had a lot I needed to do. Still, my feet made my decision for me as they followed Maverick through the halls toward the small staff room on the bottom floor of the precinct.

Chapter Twenty

Maverick

I knew the energy that Nathan was giving off. It was the same energy I gave off when Dad died and the same as Harris when he first discovered Daisy's cancer. It was the energy of a man who wanted to help but was trapped in the realization that he couldn't do anything.

I poured Nathan a coffee before taking it to the empty table Nathan had chosen to sit in.

"Alright, what's happened?"

Nathan looked up at me; distress was written all over his face. With a sigh, his eyes welled with tears. "My mum has dementia. She'd made us promise that we'd never put her into a nursing home. She wanted to die in her home. But she is getting worse, and it's too much for Dad to handle alone. Just today, she went missing for four hours. When Dad finally found her, she was swinging on the swings at the playground, in nothing but her nightgown and no underwear on."

As much as I wanted to laugh at the sight conjured in my head, I also had enough tact to know that was definitely not what was needed here.

"I can imagine how hard that is on your family. It probably doesn't help with the case you've just closed."

Nathan chuckled humourlessly. "No, that hasn't helped at all. Thankfully I'm wise enough to know that people like Sophie Haugh are a rarity."

I smiled and nodded. "That's true. I haven't had much to do with nursing facilities, but I know most staff that work in them are good people. Have you looked into getting some help in the home, maybe?"

Nathan sighed. "I don't even know where to begin."

"Your Mum's doctor hasn't given you any leads?"

Nathan shrugged and shook his head. "No, her doctor is more concerned about writing her a prescription and getting her out of there."

Wincing, I nodded. "Yeah, some of them are the worst. I have a friend, Dylan, who works for an organization called Aged Care Plus. He was really good at helping me with Dad when he was sick. He's hot, too," I snorted.

Nathan threw his head back with a laugh. "I'll keep that in mind." I didn't know what floated Nathan's boat, but my gaydar, I didn't think, was lying when I picked up that maybe he was a submissive bottom. "So, Dylan could help us keep Mum at home?"

"I don't know for sure, but he would be beneficial to talk to. He helped me to source Dad, a hospital bed, and when it came time for him to go into palliative care, Dylan could prepare it all. He organized a palliative care nurse to come and stay at the house while I was at work and take care of Dad's needs. It took so much pressure off me, and I wasn't constantly stressing."

I reached behind me and pulled my wallet from my back pocket before opening it to find where I'd stashed Dylan's card and slid it over to Nathan. "Give him a ring and see what he can do to help. But also talk to me if you need it. I know when Dad was going through everything, it was great to have Harris there to be a shoulder to cry on. I don't know if I would have survived without him."

Nathan sighed. "I don't want to be a burden on you, though. You and Harris are going through so much with his little girl."

I shook my head and reached over the table to take Nathan's. The other detective startled slightly, and I thought he might pull his hand away but instead held steady. The tears he had been fighting earlier returned and started to trek down his cheeks.

"I don't know what it is like to have a mum who is struggling with Dementia, but I know what it is like to have to deal with medical professionals and watch a loved one slowly waste away. I'm here for you.

Not just as a workmate but as a friend too. You're a good guy, Nathan, and I can see how much love you have for your Mum. Don't try to shoulder all that pressure alone; allow us and the rest of the team to take some of your burdens. Even if it is just inviting your Dad, Mum, and family to my place for dinner."

Nathan's cheeks blushed, and he released my hand to wipe his tears. "I'd be embarrassed to bring my mum around. She can be very fussy. She isn't anything like the mother I grew up with."

I nodded. "I understand that. But it is nothing to be embarrassed about. My Dad had started losing his mind only a week or so before he died. He had brain cancer, and it messed with him mentally. I was in the kitchen making a sandwich when I heard this roar and something wet slap against the living room wall." I laughed as I remembered the day and the look on the nurse's face. "I ran into the living room, wondering what was going on. The nurse had been trying to clean my father; he had started to lose control of his bowels and had to wear adult diapers. While she was cleaning him up, Dad had managed to grab hold of the diaper and hurled it at the nurse. She was lucky to have quick reflexes and dodged the shitty diaper as it hurtled through the air and slapped hard against the wall, smearing a line of shit all the way to the carpet."

I threw my head back with laughter. "Man, I was gagging so bad with the stench and laughing my ass off. The poor nurse, I felt so bad for her and tried to tell Dad off, but I couldn't; I was laughing too hard. After we got him and the shit stain cleaned up, I apologized profusely to the nurse; she told me that it wasn't the first shitty diaper she'd thrown at her, and she was skilled at dodging them now. So, don't be embarrassed. Your mum can't help what is happening to her, and she can't do anything worse than throw a shit-filled diaper at me."

Nathan chuckled. "I'm not sure she would do that. However, from what I understand from my sister, she basically flashed the entire playground today."

I snorted before covering my lips. "Sorry, man, I shouldn't laugh."

Nathan sighed and shook his head. "Don't be sorry. I need to start seeing the humor in the things she does."

"Exactly. If you don't laugh at the little things, they will slowly eat at you until you can't take it anymore."

"Thank you, Mav. You have really helped me a lot. I've got to go and see my family, and I'll tell them about Dylan; if we can get her some help while she's at home, that would be a great start."

"No worries, man, and I mean it, bring your family over for a barbecue; I'll invite Harris and his family. Derek and his wife will probably come too."

"I'd like that."

Nathan stood and turned to leave the kitchen. I smiled as I watched him go. The poor guy had a lot on his shoulders. We all had troubles, and I meant what I said to him. I wanted to help him and be there for him. We were a family, and family always stuck together.

Epilogue

ophie

    "Ms. Haugh, I really don't think it is wise for you to represent yourself," the magistrate said as she glared at me.

I shrugged my shoulders. "I'm guilty," I repeated.

The judge sighed and nodded her head. "Very well," she glanced over at the crown prosecutor. "Do you have any objections?"

"No, you're honor," the prosecutor said.

Behind me was a crowd of people, both families of those I'd taken the life of and those just yokels wanting to grab a look. Some of the media were only here because of who I was.

"Alright, I'm reminding you to the Dame Phyllis Frost Center until your sentencing, which will be held on the ninth of August."

I nodded my head and turned to face the guards that were standing by. After the judge slammed her hammer on her gavel, the guards stepped forward and took either of my arms, guiding me out of the courtroom.

"Bitch," a man snarled as I walked past him.

I looked over to see one of the children of one of the elderly patients I'd saved. I shook my head.

"I gave her peace," I replied.

The man's face instantly bloomed red with fury as he tried to stand. His wife held his arm, pulling him back into his seat.

"Move," the guard to my right barked.

I nodded and continued out of the courtroom and into the hallway. Since being remanded and waiting for my court case, I'd seen countless psychiatrists; my attorney said I needed to see them; he wanted me to plead not guilty on the grounds of insanity. I wasn't insane. I wasn't going to do that. I was guilty. I'd done what I thought was right. I'd saved those people. We'll all except Mr. Ryson. I wasn't supposed to take his life. That's why I was arrested. I'd stepped out of line.

I'd decided to fire my counsel, even though everyone told me I shouldn't. But it was stupid; he was stupid. I know he was trying to save me from prison, but even I could see there would be no getting me out of this.

Plus, the prison needed me. I saw so many lost and broken people when I walked through the doors. Women from all walks of life. So many are struggling with drug addictions, sick, vomiting, and shaking with withdrawals. They needed me.

As soon as I'd been led into the prison, I knew I had taken Mr. Ryson's life; that got me caught for a reason. I was meant to be arrested. I was told to be sent to prison. I was meant to be here.

Within the few weeks I'd been at the prison, I'd gotten work in the kitchen. I'd scoured the kitchen pantry and found Ajax cleaner. A little each time I was in there, I'd squirrel away in a small bag. The guards were pretty lax; they never checked for the powder. As soon as I had enough, it would be time.

Obviously, this was a lot cruder and probably going to cause much more painful deaths, but it was my only choice. I knew who the first would be too. Her name was Allison Rose. At one time, she would have been a beautiful woman. Still, after years of prostituting herself and chronic drug addiction, she was scarred, sick, and so sunk in her depression you could feel it oozing from her pores.

Allison admitted wanting to die but was too scared to do it herself. She told me all about her childhood. It was horrendous. She'd been passed from family member to family member, most of them nothing but filthy pedophiles who did nothing but molest her before raping her. She grew up thinking all she had worth in her life was her vagina.

It was a horrible view to have. It made me furious to think that people were so insensitive that they could do something terrible to a child. Now, Allison was forty-eight years old. Her mind was rattled; she had been reduced to a mumbling mess. Some days she was more straightforward than others, but for the most part, she was just a shell. Not too dissimilar to the Dementia patients I'd seen.

"Alright, here we are," the driver spoke. I sat in the back of the van, taking me back to the prison. My hands were cuffed in front of me, and as I stared out the window, I saw the large stone building surrounded by a wire fence and razor wire.

This was a maximum security prison for the worst of the worst. Most of the women I'd met here weren't bad people; they were victims of their circumstances. Like Tabatha, she'd killed her husband after he beat her one too many times. Some were sick bitches. But usually, they were kept away from the general population.

Like Denise Haywood. That bitch had killed all four of her children. Buckled them into their car seats and drove the car into the lake. She saved herself; she said she was planning on dying but lost her nerve. Now she was in prison. A child murderer hated.

She wasn't going to be someone that I would end, though. I liked watching her being tormented by the screams of her children every night. We would hear her screaming through the walls of the night, and it always made me smile. I wanted to see her sent crazy by her mind.

But women like Allison, they were the ones that deserved to be saved.

The van stopped, and the guard swung the door open before reaching in to take me by the cuffs.

"Take it easy on the step, Sophie," he said quietly. I smiled and nodded my head. "I heard that you fired your counsel?"

"Yes," I answered.

The guard, whose name was Neal, sighed. "I wish you wouldn't have done that. You are going to rot in here."

I shrugged my shoulders. "I think I'm where I'm supposed to be."

Neal frowned. "Are you guilty, Sophie?"

I nodded. "Oh yes. I killed all of those people. The law says that's wrong, but those people, Neal, were shells."

"I understand," Neal said with a shake of his head. "My wife died last year; she had early onset Dementia."

I smiled warmly. "Then you understand."

"I understand that we need euthanasia; I'm not sure I agree with vigilante medicine."

I chuckled. "You see it as vigilante medicine. It gives people who have lived a great life some peace."

"I guess we are just not the same."

"That's not bad; the world needs all flavors," I smiled.

Neal chuckled and nodded his head. "Yes, I guess they do. Alright, girl, come on, let's get you inside."

I smiled again and allowed Neal to lead me into my home for the foreseeable future. I'd already organized my family home to be sold and all of my finances sorted. I knew I wouldn't see the outside world again, but that was okay. I didn't need much. But what I did would help me to finish my life's work.

The End.

Don't miss out!

Visit the website below and you can sign up to receive emails whenever Samuel Davies publishes a new book. There's no charge and no obligation.

https://books2read.com/r/B-A-MQKW-MIAJC

BOOKS2READ

Connecting independent readers to independent writers.

Did you love *Retirement Killer*? Then you should read *Sisters Revenge*[1] by S L Davies!

Emmaline's twin brother, Spencer, has been found dead at a party.

The police say Spencer drowned, but Emmaline doesn't believe it. She wants the truth, and when she finds it she wants revenge.Harley and Reed, are Spencer's best friends, they want to help Emmaline find the truth, but they also want Emmaline.As the trio seek out answers they discover an unconventional love, a love that works for them.

This is a N/A book, with M/M scenes and group sex. Not suitable for under 18. It is dark and has some major triggers.

Read more at https://www.amazon.com/~/e/B0832T8F7Z.

---

1. https://books2read.com/u/mVRLg5

2. https://books2read.com/u/mVRLg5

Also by Samuel Davies

On The Hunt
On The Hunt
Always Watching
Retirement Killer

About the Author

Samuel Davies is a crime author living in Australia.